# FRESH DELICIOUS

Poems from the Farmers' Market

Irene Latham

Illustrated by Mique Moriuchi

WORDSONG

AN IMPRINT OF HIGHLIGHTS
Honesdale, Pennsylvania

For Lynn—if sisters were peaches, I'd pick you
—IL

For Isobel, Eliza, and MaryJane
—MM

WordSong
An Imprint of Highlights
815 Church Street
Honesdale, Pennsylvania 18431

Printed in China
ISBN: 978-1-62979-103-6
Library of Congress Control Number: 2015946836

First edition

Designed by Anahid Hamparian
Production by Sue Cole
The text of this book is set in Graham Regular.
The drawings are done in acrylic paints and collage.

10 9 8 7 6 5 4 3 2 1

# CONTENTS

# FARMERS' MARKET

White tents
shade truck beds
that sprout
homegrown peaks
in summertime hues.

Farmers call.
Empty baskets sway
as they wait

for tomatoes, corn,
peaches, and more.
What will
we carry home
today?

5

# TOMATO

Round like
    a baseball,

smooth like
    a balloon;

red like
    a fire truck,

ripe like
    a summer moon.

# CUCUMBERS

a fleet
of green
submarines

in a wicker
sea

# RED, YELLOW & ORANGE BELL PEPPERS

Right-side up
they shine
like ornaments

strung and hung
on a holiday
tree.

Flip them
upside down
and they

*ding-dong*
a sunset-colored
song.

# LETTUCE

I see round,
wrinkled
faces

and brows
that wear
ruffled crowns.

I touch folds
tender as
birds' wings

and fronds
ribbed like
umbrellas.

I taste butter
and pepper
and salt.

Sometimes
I crunch
into a leaf

the very
same flavor
as rain.

9

# BLUEBERRIES

Blueberries
are sweet
but not
too
sweet.

One fits
perfectly
between
finger
and thumb.

They burst
like flavor-filled
fireworks
in waffles
and muffins.

But the best
thing about
blueberries
is the way
they change

your lips
and teeth
and tongue
from regular
to purple-blue.

# CORN

I don't know
why

they call it
an *ear*

when
I see

rows
upon rows

of tiny
noses.

# ABOUT CORN

Mama says
we call them
*ears*

for the way
they grow

on the sides
of the stalk—

pert
and tufted,

tilted
away from

one
another,

listening
to the
sun.

13

# FARM-FRESH EGGS

A dozen
tiny
treasure
chests

painted
white,
brown,
or green.

Crack
open
the secret
door

and find
a trove
of farmer's
gold.

# BASIL

a bouquet
of minty
green
butterfly
wings

# PEACH

When your
baby-fuzz
cheek
meets my
hopeful nose,
the world
explodes
with sweetness.

# POTATOES

I wonder
if they know
what shape
they are?

Stub-toed,
pudgy.
Crooked as
a "come here"
finger.

I wonder
if they miss
their warm
dirt bed?

Tuck them snug
into a dark
dry drawer
so they will
feel at home.

18

# ONION

Remove
its hairy
roots,

peel its
old-man
skin.

Taste
where
it's been.

ZUCCHINI

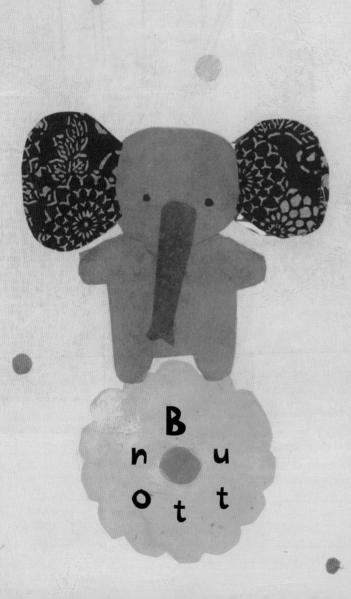

Button

1. Crookneck squash: question mark
2. Button squash: period
3. Zucchini squash: exclamation point

# PURPLE HULL PEAS

a canoe

that seats
eight or ten

green-cheeked
dark-eyed

passengers

# OKRA

a mountain
of mouse-sized
swords

stored in fuzzy
sheaths

# STRAWBERRY JAMBOREE

So many strawberries
costumed in red—

they carry green parasols
to shade their heads.

Tasteless, or tasteful?
You decide.

They wear their seeds
on the outside.

# WILD HONEY

Bee-kissed lake
displayed
in a jelly jar

tilts
and narrows
into a river—

golden drizzle
decorates
the plate;

our tongues
buzz
with pleasure.

# WATERMELON

Rind cracks,
creaks.
Reveals
a red
galaxy.

Seeds arc
out of our
mouths
like shooting
stars.

# CLOSING TIME

When our baskets
hang low and heavy

it's time to head for home.

The air throbs with recipes
as we admire our catch.

Thank you, farmers!
Thank you, earth.

Thank you, sunshine
for this fresh
          delicious
               day.

# RECIPES FROM THE FARMERS' MARKET

## COOL TOMATO-CUCUMBER-ONION SALSA

What you need:
1 large tomato
1 cucumber
¼ cup chopped onion
olive oil
balsamic vinegar
salt
pepper

Wash and dry the tomato and cucumber.
Peel the onion.
**Ask a grown-up helper** to dice the tomato, cucumber, and onion into small chunks.
Transfer to a serving bowl.
Drizzle with olive oil and a splash of balsamic vinegar.
Stir.
Add salt and pepper to taste.
Serve with tortilla chips.

## FRUIT KEBABS WITH YOGURT DIP

What you need:
any combination of fruit cut into bite-size pieces, such as watermelon, peaches, strawberries, grapes, or blueberries
wooden skewers
8 oz. carton vanilla or fruit-flavored yogurt

**Ask a grown-up helper** to cut the fruit.
Arrange the fruit on the skewers.
Alternate colors or make patterns as desired.
Spoon yogurt into small bowls for dipping.

## LETTUCE WRAPS

What you need:
*1 cucumber*
*1 tomato*
*large lettuce leaves (any variety—
  romaine works very well)*
*sliced ham*
*sliced cheese*
*prepared salad dressing, such as
  ranch or Italian*
*toothpicks*

Wash and dry the cucumber and tomato.
**Ask a grown-up helper** to slice the
  cucumber and tomato.
Line a lettuce leaf with a ham slice and a
  cheese slice.
Top with cucumber and tomato,
  as desired.
Drizzle with salad dressing.
Roll and secure with a toothpick.
Enjoy this fun sandwich alternative!

## CHEESY CONFETTI FRITTATA

What you need:
*2 tbsp. chopped onion*
*2 tbsp. chopped bell pepper*
*2 tbsp. chopped tomato*
*2 slices bacon, cooked and crumbled*
*4 oz. grated cheddar cheese*
*4 eggs*
*nonstick cooking spray*

**Ask a grown-up helper** to turn on the oven
  and chop the onion, bell pepper, and
  tomato.
Combine all ingredients except eggs in
  a bowl.
In a separate bowl, crack the eggs. Remove
  any shell bits. Whisk the eggs until blended.
Pour the contents of both bowls into an
  oven-safe dish coated with nonstick
  cooking spray. (I like to use an iron skillet.)
**Ask a grown-up helper** to bake the dish at
  400 degrees for 20 minutes, or until the
  mixture is firm.
**Ask a grown-up helper** to transfer the frittata
  to a plate.

## MINI (MANY) VEGGIE PIZZA

What you need:
diced veggies, such as bell peppers,
    tomatoes, onions, squash
plain bagels
tomato sauce
grated mozzarella cheese

**Ask a grown-up helper** to turn the oven to
    broil and chop the vegetables.
Place split bagels on a baking sheet.
Spread with the tomato sauce.
Spread the cheese evenly over the sauce.
Spoon diced vegetables onto the cheese.
**Ask a grown-up helper** to broil the pizzas
    for 10 minutes, or until the cheese is
    brown and bubbly.

## EASY STRAWBERRY* ICE CREAM

What you need:
1 quart strawberries
8 oz. carton mascarpone cheese
$\frac{1}{2}$ can (4 oz.) sweetened condensed
    milk

Wash the strawberries and remove the green
    hulls. (Softer, riper strawberries are best!)
Use a potato masher to squash the strawberries.
Add the mascarpone cheese and sweetened
    condensed milk and mash some more.
Spoon the mixture into a freezer-safe
    container.
Place in the freezer for at least 6 hours.
Enjoy with cones and sprinkles.

*This recipe can also be made with other
fruits, such as raspberries, ripe bananas, or
peeled peaches.